Biff and Chip went to school.
They went with Wilf and Wilma.

1

Biff and Chip liked Mrs May.
They were in her class.

Wilf liked Mrs May. He was in her class too.

It was story time.

The story was The Wizard of Oz.
It was about a girl and her dog.

The girl was Dorothy.

There was a storm. The wind
blew the house away.

Dorothy met the Scarecrow.
She met the Tin Man. She met
the Lion.

Dorothy met a witch.

There was a storm. It was
playtime.

The children couldn't play
outside.

The children played inside. They played The Wizard of Oz.

Mrs May liked the little play.

Mrs May put on a play. The play
was The Wizard of Oz.

Wilf's mum helped Mrs May.

Chip was the Tin Man. Wilf was
the Lion.

Biff was a witch.

Wilf's dad helped Mrs May. He
painted a house.

The children helped him.

The mums and dads came. They
liked the play.

"What a good play!" they said.

The children liked the play. They
gave Mrs May some flowers.

"It was good fun," said Wilf.

It was time to go home. There
was a storm.
"It's like the play," said Chip.